Third Grade Outsider

Meet Me, Brix Wilder

By: Marcy Blesy

Illustrated by: Thomas Roth

Illustrations by Thomas Roth

Cover design by Cormar Covers

Follow my blog for information about upcoming books or short stories.

Sunday, August 31

What's Up?

Hi. It's me, Brix—*Brix Wilder*. I know you know me, but someday someone might find this book, and that someone needs to know my first *and* last name. Plus, I have a cool name. I think it's cool anyway. Teachers don't think it's cool. Teachers see *Wilder* on their class list and think, **"Oh no, not that Wilder kid."** But that's not fair. I didn't choose my last name. That was my parent's fault.

Plus, what happened in second grade was not my fault, either. I mean, I DID dump the lunch table on the last day of school. But the janitor forgot to put the lock on the table. So,

3

when I leaned on it, the other side bent up. Apples and fruit cups and juice boxes went flying. It was cool—like a rainbow lunch. Mr. Harris must not like rainbows. He made me miss all of my recess to help Mr. Ollie clean the floor. Mr. Ollie kept mumbling to himself, *I hate this job. I hate this job.* I totally understand.

Tomorrow is the first day of third grade. I know this year will be better. I can feel it in my bones. And I really can because my bones have gotten bigger over the summer. At my physical, the doctor said I grew two inches and have bones like a basketball player. Pretty soon I will be able to catch my bird, Willa, when she gets free and sits on the curtain rod. I won't have to call in my sisters for help. They all have long bones, too. I'm the youngest *and* the shortest in my family of six. But put me up against any of my classmates, and I'm the tallest. Maybe I can bring Willa to school this year. When she gets loose, Mrs. Cooper will say, "Brix, could you please use your long legs and long arms to reach that wonderful bird and put her back in her cage?" I will be the hero. That sounds like a great way to make Mrs. Cooper like me. I'm tired of being the WILDER outsider kid.

It's time for bed now. Mom says I need eight hours of good sleep to be at my best. Night all.

Monday after school, September 1

What's Up?

Hello from the end of the first day of school at Western Oaks Elementary School. Whew! What a day! It started great. I woke up after my eight hours of sleep. My big sisters, Aspen, Sutten, and Kristen, were eating breakfast at the same time. I couldn't believe my luck. I got the bathroom all to myself. That *never* happens.

I was happily washing my armpits, humming my favorite Jonas Brothers song. That's when the trouble began. *Pound. Pound. Pound.* **"Get out of the bathroom, Brix Wilder."** It was my sister Aspen. She's the oldest. And the loudest. And the one who thinks she's the boss of the world.

I had to finish first. I couldn't go to school with one stinky armpit. **"Wait your turn!"** I told her.

But then my sister Sutten showed up. Sutten is a prima donna. That's what my dad called her the last time he was home. She needs the most time to get ready. She's always the last one in the car. I don't understand. Her hair is long and straight. Why does it take so long to brush hair like that? Maybe it's all the makeup she wears that takes time. I don't know much about makeup except that when you cry, it turns your face black. That happens to Sutten, too. She cries a lot—usually about boys. Aspen doesn't wear makeup. She's too busy playing sports to put on makeup.

I was going to open the bathroom door when my sister Kristen started screaming. "I have to pee! Let me in!" Everyone knows that when Kristen screams, she won't stop until she gets what she wants.

Aspen was pounding. Sutten was talking about running out of time. Kristen was screaming about needing to use the toilet. So much for the start to the perfect day.

I slowly opened the door. My sisters were a totem pole of heads stacked on top of each other. I determined my best strategy. As soon as they started climbing over each other to get into the bathroom, I ducked behind the statue of sisters, slinked against the wall, and ran downstairs for breakfast. *Safe.* I really should play more baseball. I bet I could steal a base better than anyone else on the team.

Mom looked stressed. It was her first day of school, too. She was moving from being a sixth-grade teacher to an eighth-grade teacher. Even though she had taught since I was a baby, she said switching grades was like starting all over. I felt that way, too. Being a third grader is a lot different than being a second grader.

I emptied the cereal box into my bowl. I had to shake out what was left—fifteen little circles—FIFTEEN. I guess Mom forgot to buy new cereal for the first week of school. She forgets a lot when

Dad is gone. He is the remember parent in the family.

I knew better than to complain, so I ate my fifteen pieces of cereal and half a banana I found on the counter. Probably Sutten ate the other half. She never finishes her food.

A horn started honking outside. It was my ride—Mr. Wheeler, Marlow and Grady's dad. He has been my ride to school for years. Marlow and Grady are my best friends. They are twins. Marlow is a girl. Grady is a boy. Mr. Wheeler used to take Kristen to school, too, but this year she is in the middle school, so Mom will take her to school. Kristen is going to miss out on our burping contests. She's surprisingly talented in the burp department. Aspen drives Sutten to the high school. Having a sister that can drive helps Mom out, too. When Dad has a tour of duty for the Army, it's hard on all of us. He won't be home until after Christmas.

I wanted to brush my teeth. Having banana breath is like having a paper towel wadded up in your mouth—mushy, gross. But I wasn't about to try to get back in the bathroom. **"Have a good day, Mom!"** I yelled. If Dad had been here he would have remembered to take first day of school pictures. That's okay. Gotta run.

Monday late night, September 1

What's Up?

I'm back. I want to finish telling you about my day. My sisters are watching videos on Aspen's phone in her room. I can hear them laughing from my room. I can hear everything from my room— because I don't even really have a bedroom. By the time I came along, my house was full. Mom and Dad put my crib at the end of the hallway under the pulldown attic stairs. When I learned to climb out of the crib when I was fifteen months old (since I've heard this story a million times), they put a gate across the hall. It's like I was in baby jail. Now there is a wooden screen there instead of a gate. At least I can change my clothes in privacy. But noise? Well, I hear EVERYTHING!

Back to my day—Marlow, Grady, and I are in the same class. We were so excited to see our names on Mrs. Cooper's class list. Mr. Wheeler dropped us off in the car lane. We said goodbye quickly. If we take too much time, the parents still in line get really mad and start honking. Last year my dad had to take me to school during the week Marlow and Grady had the flu. He got honked at every day. He always wanted to give Kristen and me big hugs. Kristen was super embarrassed. I didn't mind too much. (Plus, I don't want to hurt Dad's feelings when he gets home and reads my book. He's the reason I write this stuff. I don't want him to miss a thing while he's away at work.

He loves to hear my stories.)

Marlow and Grady walked into Mrs.
Cooper's room first. I walked in backwards behind
them. I was once chased by a monster. I like to
watch my back whenever I can. Everyone tells me

that the monster was just a really big dog from down the block. All I know is that thing had giant teeth with massive black eyes and long brown hair. I've never seen a dog that looked like that before. Ever since I started walking backwards into rooms or buildings, I have not been chased again.

Foster Huttley was the first person I saw when I turned around. I groaned out loud. He heard me. I know that because he gave me the stink eye—a scrunched-up face look. I get that all the time from my sisters. I am immune to the stink eye. It doesn't bother me at all.

The second person I saw was Kensington Morris. She goes by Kensi unless she's trying to act better than she is. Then she says, **"My name is**

KENSINGTON!" Usually, I roll my eyes when she does that. Kensi didn't give me the stink eye. She made a noise with her lips—kind of like when you learn to swim and blow bubbles in the water. I think it was meant to annoy me. It didn't.

Mrs. Cooper told us to find our desks. My desk was in the back of the room. Thinking about it, I wonder if she did that on purpose. Maybe Mr. Harris told her I would make trouble. It's not like I mean to cause trouble. My dad says I'm an outsider. I think that's a good thing, though. I think "outside the box," not like "outside" with trees and grass and flowers and stuff. I think "outside" of what everyone else is thinking. I'm myself—Brix Wilder. And sometimes my thinking looks like trouble to other people—like Mr. Harris. If my rainbow pen could show you my thoughts on my second grade teacher Mr. Harris, it would start jumping up and down because he gave me the heebie jeebies. He just didn't understand my outsider specialness. Dad told me that, too.

Mrs. Cooper is a lot nicer than Mr. Harris. All three of my sisters had her. That's good and bad. They were mostly good students but also full of drama. They are still full of drama—always having trouble with friends, and now my biggest sisters have trouble with boys. I don't make drama. I'm also not the best student—except in writing. You can clearly see that I am the best writer. That's because of Mom. She has been making me write since I was little. "I will not shampoo Aunt Jan's dog. I will not shampoo Aunt Jan's dog. I will not shampoo Aunt Jan's dog." I wrote over and over and over until she thought I understood. Or, there was the time she made me write a letter to the mailman after I put baby toads in the mailbox. They like dark, quiet places, right? I guess not everyone agreed. That time I had to write a letter to the mailman.

Dear Mr. Kindle,

I am sorry you did not like the toads in the mailbox. I thought they could live there in peace. That went away when you screamed. They were probably glad to go to the pond instead. That's where Mom made me take them. Anyway, sorry

I scared you.

From,

Brix

At least that's how I remember the letter. It was a long time ago, though.

I also had to write a whole paper about why I'm lucky to have sisters. That was really hard, and I don't want to remember it all. The only good thing about that time was that Mom made my sisters write a paper about why they were lucky to have a little brother. They got to write their paper together. That was not fair at all. Plus, she EDITED my paper. I got this whole speech from her about learning from my mistakes. I am a talented writer, though.

Anyway, Mrs. Cooper is going to be knocked right out of her socks when she sees how well I can write. Notice how I said *well* and not *good*. That's because I use correct grammar, too.

We had to play a get-to-know-you game. I know most of the kids. I didn't know who likes peas, who went to the ocean for summer vacation, or who read twenty books, though. Those were some of the questions we had to find kids to answer. Grady answered five of the questions on my paper. Marlow answered four. Mrs. Cooper told us we had to ask other kids the rest of the questions. We split up. I steered clear of Kensi and Foster. I tapped on the shoulder of a boy who was half my size. When he turned around he was looking just above my belly button. That made me giggle. **"What's so funny?"** he asked me. I had to think of a lie real quick. I told him I imagined Mrs. Cooper wearing a bumblebee costume. I admit it wasn't a great lie, but I'd just seen a big bee fly in from the open window, and that's the first thing that came to my mind. The boy smiled. **"I'm Teddy,"** he said. **"Like the bear?"** I asked. I know. I know. It was not a nice thing to say. Sometimes things just pop into my mind. Then they explode out of my mouth faster than a baseball flying out of an MLB pitcher's mitt. I quickly asked Teddy if he went fishing over the summer. He said "yes." I wrote his name on my paper and moved along.

After our get-to-know-you game, Mrs. Cooper passed out textbooks. We got one for Language Arts, Math, Science, and Social Studies.

We also got a spelling workbook, a math workbook, and a science journal. That's a crazy amount of books. After I added the books to my desk with my new colored pencils, markers, and crayons, it was so full I could barely shut the lid. Third grade is serious business.

She gave us all fish crackers for a snack. In second grade we got seven crackers—seven exactly because I always counted. The one day I got six crackers, I was sure to let Mr. Harris know. "Uhh...Uhh..." I cleared my throat a bunch of times. I was trying to be quiet about it. It's not like it was a world tragedy, but when you are a growing boy and your body is used to seven fish crackers and you only get six, it IS a matter worth pursuing.

Finally, I just had to go for it. I stood up and said, "Mr. Harris, there is a little problem here." I pointed at my desk. He looked at the six fish crackers on my desk. It was an obvious problem with an obvious solution. He didn't blink once—or say a thing. "I need another fish cracker. I only got six." That's when Kensi opened her loud mouth. "He ate a cracker already, Mr. Harris. I saw him." She smiled at me so big the reflection off her braces was blinding. "Be thankful for what you have, Mr. Wilder. There are starving children in the world." When Mr. Harris pulled the "starving children in the world" words out of his head and through his mouth, I lost it. "Kensi is a big fat liar!" I didn't mean she was "fat" like her clothes were too tight "fat"—just that her mouth was fat with lies. But Mr. Harris didn't listen to my arguments. He sent me to the office to cool down. And I never got to eat ANY of my fish crackers that day!

But it's a new year. And Mrs. Cooper gave us each ten fish crackers. It was awesome! Third grade is so much cooler than second grade.

The last thing we did was get our homework. Most kids groaned and moaned. Not me. I love homework. Plus, the project she assigned sounds super cool. We have to fill a paper bag with five things that describe us. We can use pictures, objects, food, or whatever we can think of. She said we should "be creative." It's due on Wednesday. I wish Dad could help me with this project. It's super important to choose the perfect items to describe me. I want everyone in third grade to GET me.

Then it was time to go—only a half day on the first day of school. Mr. Wheeler brought me home. I let out a big burp as a thank you. Aspen and Sutten were already home. All of my sisters spent the night complaining about first day homework. But I am not going to let them bring me down. This is the year of Brix.

Tuesday morning, September 2

What's Up?

I am writing before school because I have to tell you right away about something that happened last night. Mom was super cranky. I guess she has a really rowdy group of eighth graders this year. Plus, Dad was supposed to call from Germany, but he didn't. Sometimes he has to do work right away since he's a Captain in the Army. Then he can't call because Germany is six hours ahead of us. Mom likes her private talks with dad. Sometimes I hear her cry. Sometimes I hear her talk nonstop— usually about my sisters. I don't cause any trouble. Well, I guess you know that's a lie, but I don't listen when she talks about me.

I tried to cheer Mom up, so I decided to make a special dessert after dinner. Chocolate cheers everyone up, right? I opened the kitchen cabinets first. I get inspired that way. I pulled out a box of brownie mix. I read the back. That's super responsible. I know, you are impressed. I got two eggs out of the refrigerator. I also grabbed the vegetable oil from the top of the pantry shelf. It's helpful to be so tall. I didn't even need a chair to reach it. I mixed everything up with Mom's mixing spoon. I sprayed nonstick spray on the pan, set the temperature on the oven, and slid the brownies right inside. Everyone would be so proud of me! And everyone would be in a happy mood.

But, that's when the trouble started. Aspen screamed first. Then Sutten. Then Kristen. Mom thundered upstairs. I followed. All of the girls were standing on Aspen's bed and pointing. "What is going on?" Mom asked. "What's wrong?" I asked. "There's—a—mouse under the dresser!" Sutten shrieked. She waved her hands over her face in a regular Sutten way. "I'll get a hammer!" yelled Kristen. Mom looked from girl to girl to girl to me. She shook her head NO over and over. Then I got a lightbulb idea. "I have an idea!" I said. "I'm getting a hammer!" Kristen said again. Mom chased Kristen out of the room while Aspen and Sutten stood hugging each other on the bed. I ran into the living room. My National Geographic Channel training kicked in. Birds hunt rodents. I have a bird. There was a rodent in my sister's bedroom. Willa jumped on my finger. She loves to be out of her cage. I had the perfect solution. But as soon as we reached Aspen's room, I realized maybe I was wrong. Aspen and Sutten were screaming again. I saw the mouse at the same time Willa did. But instead of hunting the mouse, she flew circles around my sisters dive-bombing at their heads. I know why. She was telling them to BE QUIET! BE QUIET! BE QUIET! But they don't talk bird like I do. Sutten threw her arms out to protect her face. Willa went flying across the room when Sutten struck her with her flimsy arms.

Willa hit the wall and slid down to the ground. It was pathetic! Poor Willa! Then I screamed! It was my turn, after all. Mom solved all the problems. She always does when Dad's not here to help. She ordered Aspen and Sutten off the bed. She ordered Kristen to get a mouse trap and to set it in the hallway. She ordered me to stop screaming. She picked up Willa with a towel. She put her in a shoebox. I poked holes in the lid so she could breathe. We drove to the veterinarian's office. The vet looked her over. He said she was just in shock. She will be fine, but we have to give her some quiet and cover her cage.

Mom had calmed down by the time she turned our car onto our street. That's when I realized why it had been so quiet. Mom must have left her cell phone at home. Otherwise, my sisters would have been texting the whole time about that silly mouse. I wish I'd lived in the time of no internet. I was thinking this when a fire truck turned onto the street behind us. The sirens were blaring. And when a fire truck is close, it's REALLY loud. Mom pulled over. I was in a trance from staring at the lights when Mom yelled, **"Oh no!"** She sped down the rest of our street. **"Oh no!"** I yelled, too, when I saw the fire truck sitting in front of our house and my sisters running around our yard.

Since I have to get to school, I'll summarize for you. In all that trouble with the mouse and Willa, I forgot about the surprise brownies in the oven. It really did turn out to be quite a surprise after all. The kitchen filled with smoke. The brownies were burnt to near ashes. There was never any fire, so I'm not sure why Mom was as mad at me as she was. But I guess getting smoke smell out of a house is going to take a long time and a lot of money. So, this morning I am writing to you from a hotel room that I shared with my three sisters, Mom, and one angry bird who wasn't getting the quiet the vet ordered. All three of my sisters said, **"Can't you ever do anything right, Brix?"** I'm not going to lie. It hurt my feelings. I wish Dad was home. Let's hope the school day goes better.

Tuesday night, September 2

What's Up?

Tonight, I am staying at Grady and Marlow's house. Mom didn't think it was such a good idea for us all to stay in a hotel for another night. I could not agree more. Sleeping with Kristen's foot in my face all night was not fun. The house is being professionally cleaned, whatever that means. I have one problem being away from home, though. Our paper bag project is due tomorrow. All of my things I was going to use are in my house—which I can't go to right now. Grady and Marlow said we would figure something out later.

First, I want to tell you about school. We had recess for the first time this year. Our playground is big. We have a bunch of moms and dads who organized a running fundraiser when I was in kindergarten. Every kid asked adults they knew to pledge money. All us kids had to do was run around and around the football field. Then we collected the money. The moms and dads raised over $20,000, which sounds like a lot of money. They bought new playground equipment. There is this spinner toy. You sit on it, and it spins around and around and around. I like it because I like to feel dizzy. Most people don't, but I'm not like most people. Anyway, even with all of the new equipment, the holey tree is still the most popular hangout. It's not holey like church kind of holy. It's called the holey tree because there is a giant opening in the bottom of this gigantic tree. The hole makes the perfect scoop seat for your butt. And Foster Huttley's butt sits in that spot the most. Hutt's Butt Chair is what all his friends call it. I've never sat there myself, though I would like to.

Well, today at our first recess of third grade, there was a big problem. Teddy sat in the holey tree. Marlow saw it first. **"Oh no!"** she said. **"Teddy is in Hutt's Butt Chair."** It was like the entire playground saw it at the same time. Everyone seemed to freeze faster than an ice cube in the North Pole. I knew we had to help Teddy. It wasn't his fault. He didn't know that Foster ruled the playground. "**Stay out of it,**" said Grady to me. He pulled the back of my shirt. But I am stronger than I look. I started jogging when I saw Foster walking to the tree, too.

"Hey, Foster!" I said. "Want to swing?" He stopped for a second. He glared at me. Lasers shot out of his eyeballs. Well, not really, but it seemed like it. He shoved me out of his way. **"Hey, kid! That's my seat!"** yelled Foster. Teddy's eyeballs got as big as dinner plates. He backed up as far as he could go. If the tree could have eaten him up, I think he would have let it at that moment. I just acted. I didn't think first. I have that habit. I jumped in between Foster and Teddy. I threw my arms out as wide as I could. **"Hey, guys! Let me make an introduction. This is Foster's Hutt Butt Chair. Teddy, you can find another spot on the playground. I'll help you find it. Come on."** I thought I solved the problem. Foster stopped in his tracks. He lowered the fist he had raised. Except I was wrong because Teddy didn't budge.

He said, "I was here first." Now, no one could argue with his logic. He WAS in the tree seat first. But Foster owned that spot. No one can really remember why he was the one who took ownership of the spot—probably because he was big and mean and his butt fit perfectly there. And no one had ever challenged him before—until today. The whole school held their breath. Even the squirrels and the birds stopped chattering. Then the whistle blew. Foster and Teddy were the last ones to line up. I have to say I admire that kid. It's hard enough being the new kid, let alone standing up to one of the school bullies on the first full day of school.

Grady and Marlow thought I was crazy to get involved. I said I would have been crazy not to get involved. I know what it's like to be picked on. I was doing my duty to try to protect Teddy. That's also why I walked into the classroom backwards behind Teddy but in front of Foster—keeping an eye on the enemy.

Foster didn't forget about recess. Mrs. Cooper asked me to pass out the spelling lists. When I got to his desk, he stuck his foot out. I'm not dumb. I saw his foot, so I stepped around it, but what I didn't know was that Kensi was passing behind me at the same time. She had just filled her water bottle. When I backed into her, she dropped her water bottle. Water flew everywhere, including on the stack of spelling words. I looked at the words. The ink on the words started to blur. POOR became POOP. COOKING turned to COOTIES. I knew Mrs. Cooper would not be happy. "You—you, stupid boy!" yelled Kensi. "Don't call my friend stupid!" yelled Grady. "Looks like Brix can't stay out of trouble today," said Foster. "Go back to second grade. You're too young to be here. You don't belong in third grade," said Kensi. That was a low blow. I AM young. My parents got special permission to put me in school a little early. Mom said it was because she was a teacher and that I was really smart. I think it was because they were tired of paying for childcare for me. Thank goodness I am tall for my age. At least I look like I belong in third grade. But the truth is that I haven't turned eight yet. I won't turn eight until the end of September. Everyone knows it, too, because my mom makes a big deal out of my birthday every year. She sends in cupcakes and balloons. And after the kids sing Happy Birthday, they say, **"Are you one? Are you two? Are you three?"** When they stop at the right number, they all giggle because some of the kids are a full year older than me. Grady and Marlow don't laugh, even though they are some of the kids who are a full year older.

By this time, Mrs. Cooper noticed the trouble. She sighed. She didn't yell at me, but the

46

"I'm disappointed in you, Brix" look was worse than yelling. Maybe I really don't belong in third grade.

Tuesday late night, September 2

What's Up?

Grady, Marlow, and I played video games tonight. They have a super cool racing game. I even won once. Mrs. Wheeler made chocolate chip cookies. I am happy here. I don't feel like an outsider. Good night.

Wednesday before school, September 3

What's Up?

Today is a big day. I am turning in my paper bag project. We stayed up late after eating cookies. Grady and Marlow made their bags easily. This is what Grady put in his bag:

*a rubber fish (because he loves fishing)

*a picture of his grandpa (because he loves his grandpa)

*a baby picture of him and Marlow (because being a twin is pretty cool)

*a baseball (because it's his favorite sport)

*a potato (because of French fries—duh!)

This is what Marlow put in her bag:

*a hairbrush (because she has super, tangly hair)

*a picture of her and Grady at Disney World (because of the twin thing)

*a box of spaghetti (because it's her favorite food)

*a fake painting by Van Gogh (because she loves art, and he is cool because he cut off his ear)

*a stuffed giraffe (her favorite animal in the world)

I called Mom to see if I could get some stuff out of my hallway room. She said I couldn't—the house is still airing out. So, Grady and Marlow let me use anything they had that might describe me. I want people to really understand me. That's important in third grade. The first thing I put in my bag was a picture of my family even though they can be annoying. Since I didn't have a real picture, I had to be creative. I took Mrs. Wheeler's old design magazines and cut out pictures of three girls, a boy, a mom, and a dad. Finding the dad took a long time. I wanted to find a dad in a military uniform because that's a cool thing about my dad. The second thing I found was a ruler because I'm super tall. That makes me different and describes me well. Third, I took one sock from Grady and one sock from Marlow and put them together. Mom is always yelling at me for wearing mismatched socks. Being mixed up can be cool. Fourth, I put Grady's third place baseball trophy in my bag because I have one just like it at home. Even though the whole team has the same trophy, no one on that team struck out more than me—FIVE TIMES! I also got a home run. A random runaway dog on the field MAY have distracted the other team when I hit that dribbler a foot away from home plate, but it still counted as a homerun after I ran around all the bases! Finally, I dropped my rainbow pen in the bag. I won't use anything but this rainbow pen to write. It belongs to Dad. He told me to take care of his favorite pen. I won't let him down. I'm dependable. I have to go now. Mr. Wheeler has given us the five-minute countdown to his wheels backing out of the driveway for school. Until tonight…

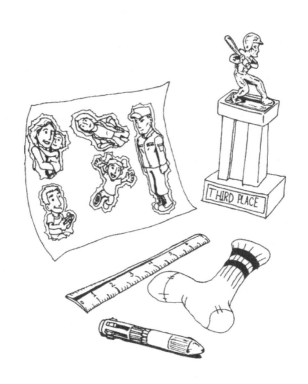

Wednesday night, September 3

What's Up?

Wow! What a day! Five great things happened today. It was the best Wednesday of the first week of school ever. One, we showed our paper bags at school. Kensi went first, of course. She brought:

*a tiara (some kind of crown thing)

*a crystal egg (from some weird collection— though I'm not sure if she collects crystals or eggs)

*a *Save the Whales* shirt (though we don't live anywhere near an ocean)

*a picture of her mom and dad who both play the violin in an orchestra

*a boring apple

I was yawning by the time she finished. She adds more words to sentences than a fast-talking salesman. Foster brought easy things:

*a chocolate bar

*a mini basketball

*a tennis racket

*a football

*a picture of his grandma who was on the first female soccer team at our local college. Come to think of it, that one was pretty cool.

After Grady and Marlow shared their bags, Mrs. Cooper said it was time for recess. That's when the second-best thing of the day happened.

The first thing I did on the playground was look for Teddy. He wasn't in the Butt Chair—

Foster sat proudly in his spot. "Where do you think he went?" asked Marlow. "I don't know," said Grady. That's when I saw him. I pointed. "Up there!" Sure enough, that kid had CLIMBED Foster Huttley's tree. He sat on a branch directly above him but hidden by the leaves—except for his legs that swang over the edge just above Foster. I looked around. None of the teacher's saw him. Neither did Foster because every few seconds, an acorn or stick would DROP out of the tree and land on top of Foster. It was awesome. Grady, Marlow, and I had to look away so Foster wouldn't see us laugh. But we also knew that pretty soon, Foster would look up. And who knows what he'd do if he spied Teddy. Grady, Marlow, and I walked over to Foster. "Want to play basketball?" we asked. "With YOU?" he moaned. "Yes, with us. We need a point guard. You're our man. I'll play center because—you know—the tallness." I pointed at my body. Marlow giggled. Foster looked skeptical. Then Grady tossed him the basketball, and he got up. He followed Grady and Marlow to the basketball court. I hung back a second. Without looking up, I said, "Hey, Teddy. Cool hiding spot. Just be careful because if Foster finds you, there are no number of trees that can protect you." Teddy didn't say anything, but I imagined him smiling.

After recess, it was my turn to show my bag.
There were a few laughs when I showed my
mixed-up, cut-out family. I tried to ignore that. I
looked at Marlow. She smiled. I continued. Mrs.
Cooper REALLY liked my mismatched socks.
"That happens all the time to me, too, Brix," she

said. "I think they just stink," said Kensi. She plugged her nose. But that was stupid. They were CLEAN socks. I was showing Grady's/my baseball trophy, when the third best thing of the day happened. There was a knock at the door. Mrs. Cooper peeked through the door blinds. She stepped outside. There was some whispering in the hallway. When she came back, my MOM was following her. I was shocked—and a little embarrassed. I am too old to have my mommy showing up unannounced at school. I forgave her right away, though, because of what she was carrying—WILLA'S CAGE! The cage was covered, but I knew what was inside. I was super confused as to why Willa was at school. She set

Willa's cage down and walked over to me. She got close and whispered in my ear. "I brought Willa for your paper bag project. I thought you might like to show her since she's pretty special to you." I really wanted to hug my Mom, but again, there's that being too old to hug your mom in public thing. "Looks like you are just in time, Mrs. Wilder. Brix, would you like to finish showing your bag?" I walked to the cage. I picked it up. "And the last thing I would like to show you is my bird, Willa." I pulled the blanket off the top. Willa was sitting on her perch. She whistled when she saw me. Everybody laughed. She didn't look like she was in shock anymore from her accident. Mom smiled.

Since it was the end of the school day, Mom took me with her. We went to get ice cream. That was the fourth best thing of the day. "How'd you get out of work to bring Willa to my school?" I asked. "I had to meet the insurance people at our house after things were cleaned from the smoke damage. I took the afternoon off." I nodded my head. "I like it when you pick me up." She smiled again. "Brix, I know you were trying to do a good thing the other night—with the brownies, I mean." I nodded again. "I didn't mean to smoke up the kitchen." She squeezed my hand. "I know. Also, I have some good news." I waited for her to tell me. "Dad is coming home early from Germany," she said. I knocked entire backpack on the floor of the car. Papers spilled out everywhere. I didn't even care. Five great things in one day tops any other day I have ever had in my life. Third grade is going to be the best year yet.

Thank you for reading, *Third Grade Outsider, Meet Me, Brix Wilder*

Please consider leaving a review on Amazon. Thank you.

Books 2 and 3 in the *Third Grade Outsider* series will be published in Summer 2020.

Thank you to Chris, Anne, and Michael for your thoughtful comments. As always, you are immensely helpful. Thank you, Tom, for your wonderful illustrations that complemented this book so perfectly.

Ed, Connor, and Luke, thank you for your support and love.

**MB

I want to thank my parents, Mayo and Liz, for helping me through tough times. I want to thank Kyle, Megan, Zach, and Alyssa for enjoying my art. I also want to thank my co-workers at Blossomland Learning Center for all the positive vibes they have sent my way.

**TR

Other Children's Books by Marcy Blesy:

Clara and Tuni, Softball Swings

There are two things that nine-year-old Clara can count on when her family moves to a new town. One, her love for trying new sports will help her meet people. Two, her friendship with her pet unicorn Tuni means she will never be alone. However, a sudden fear of swinging the bat might end Clara's softball career soon after it begins.

Clara and Tuni, Volleyball Serves

There are two things that nine-year-old Clara can count on when her family moves to a new town. One, her love for trying new sports will help her meet people. Two, her friendship with her pet unicorn Tuni means she will never be alone. However, learning how each person plays a special role on the volleyball team means that Clara must also learn to shine despite hurting feelings of a teammate.

Clara and Tuni, Basketball 1-2-3, Team!

Niles and Bradford, Baseball Bully

There are two things that nine-year-old Niles can count on when his family moves to a new town. One, his love for trying new sports will help him meet people. Two, his friendship with his pet dragon Bradford means he will never be alone. However, when a bully on the baseball team makes life hard for Niles, Bradford's idea of helping his friend gets him banned from the game.

Niles and Bradford, Basketball Shots

There are two things that nine-year-old Niles can count on when his family moves to a new town. One, his love for trying new sports will help him meet people. Two, his friendship with his pet dragon Bradford means he will never be alone. However, when things do not go as well as planned during an important basketball game, Niles starts to doubt himself.

Niles and Bradford, Soccer Kicks

Niles and Bradford, Track Team

Niles and Bradford, Flag Football Fumbles

Evie and the Volunteers Series

Join ten-year-old Evie and her friends as they volunteer all over town meeting lots of cool people and getting into just a little bit of trouble. There is no place left untouched by their presence, and what they get from the people they meet is greater than any amount of money.

Dax and the Destroyers: (a new *Evie and the Volunteers spin-off featuring a popular character)*

Book 1:   House Flip

Twelve-year-old Dax spends the summer with his Grandma. When a new family moves into the run-down house across the street, Dax finds a fast friend in their son Harrison. Not to be outdone by his friends, Evie and the Volunteers, and all of their good deeds, Dax finds himself immersed in the business of house flipping as well as Harrison's family drama. But don't expect things to go smoothly when Evie and her friends get word of this new volunteer project. Everyone has an opinion about flipping this house.

Book 2:   Park Restoration

Be the Vet:

Do you like dogs and cats?

Have you ever thought about being a veterinarian?

Place yourself as the narrator in seven unique stories about dogs and cats. When a medical emergency or illness impacts the pet, you will have the opportunity to diagnose the problem and suggest treatment. Following each story is the treatment plan offered by Dr. Ed Blesy, a 20-year practicing veterinarian. You will learn veterinary terms and diagnoses while being entertained with fun, interesting stories.

Also available:

Be the Vet 2

What's it Like to Be the Vet?

For ages 9-12

Am I Like My Daddy?

Join seven-year-old Grace on her journey through coping with the loss of her father while learning about the different ways that people grieve the loss of a loved one. In the process of learning about who her father was through the eyes of others, she learns about who she is today because of her father's personality and love. Am I Like My Daddy? is a book designed to help children who are coping with the loss of a loved one. Children are encouraged to express through journaling what may be so difficult to express through everyday conversation. Am I Like My Daddy? teaches about loss through reflection.

Am I Like My Daddy? is an important book in the children's grief genre. Many books in this genre deal with the time immediately after a loved one dies. This book focuses on years after the death, when a maturing child is reprocessing his or her grief. New questions arise in the child's need to fill in those memory gaps.

Made in the USA
Middletown, DE
03 August 2020

14461110R00046